W9-AAG-703

# Sheryl St. Germain

# How Heavy
# the Breath of God

University of North Texas Press

10 9 8 7 6 5 4 3 2


Permissions

University of North Texas Press
Post Office Box 13856
Denton, Texas 76203-3856


Library of Congress Cataloging-in-Publication Data

St. Germain, Sheryl, 1954—
How heavy the breath of God : poems / Sheryl St. Germain.
    p.        cm.        — (Texas poets series ; no. 5.)
                ISBN 0-929398-68-8
                I. Title. II. Series
PS3569. T1223H69                         1994
811'. 54—dc20                                    93-34833
                                                        CIP

The paper used in this book meets the minimum requirements of
the American National Standard for Permanence of Paper for
Printed Library materials, z39.48.1984. Binding materials have
been chosen for durability.


Cover art *Ik*, (Mayan) God of Storms with cartouche
by Carol Cullar

Jacket design by Aaron Pendland

*I.*

*What gives value to travel is fear. It is the fact that, at a
certain moment, when we are so far from our own country
. . . we are seized by a vague fear, and an instinctive desire
to go back to the protection of old habits. . . . At that moment we are porous, so that the slightest touch makes us
quiver to the depths of our being. We come across a cascade
of light, and there is eternity. . . . There is no pleasure in
traveling. . . . Pleasure takes us away from ourselves in the
same way as distraction, in Pascal's use of the word, takes
us away from God. Travel, which is like a greater and
graver science, brings us back to ourselves.*

—*Albert Camus, Notebooks 1935–1942*

I would like to acknowledge
The National Endowment for the Arts, the Texas Institute
of Letters and The University of Texas at Austin. An NEA
Fellowship, and the Dobie-Paisano Fellowship
co-sponsored by TIL and UT Austin provided me with the
support necessary to complete the
manuscript for this book.


Acknowledgement is due the following journals and
anthologies, where some of these poems made their first
appearance: *Bloomsbury Review, Calyx, The Dallas Review,
Five Fingers Review, High Plains Literary
Review, New Letters, RiverSedge, The Guadalupe Review,* and
*New Texas '91.*

*For the jungles, waters and wildlife of South America—*
*this book is a prayer*

# Contents

*II.*

## ◉◉ *Looking for Grace in Ecuador*

I am looking for the archangels
of my childhood, their pink
fleshy wings like candy,
the nimbuses of saints, gold as pollen,
the holy mothers of children,
the carpenter fathers,
I am looking into the soupy
eyes of dirty children,
god strapped to their backs,
I am looking for the grace
to wash sight away.

## ◎◎ *Street Market, Otavalo*

The first thing you notice is
the air smells different
and you are afraid of the smell
of street and rain and exhaustion
and the large weeping of mountains

and the ancient sidewalks
with their ancient smells and ancient cracks
and pools of water that smell
like broken pieces of lives,

so you step over the pools
afraid to look in them
and still there is the smell
ever rich ever growing,
feather and chicken tied for selling
smell of blood and meat,
the stripped flesh hung from hooks
in the street like tapestries
and boiling chicken smell in the stalls
and roasting pig and guinea pig and lemons

and bananas and limes
and the smell of wool, fresh
and damp and older than you
will ever be, and there is breath
and skin and color everywhere.

And you stay outside of it for awhile,
afraid of the colors and the faces
too pure, dark as those pools
of standing water in the broken
sidewalk you will not look at,
and then you see your own face
in a window, pale and washed out
as your life seems, less than a shadow,
but still you are afraid
to breathe too deeply for fear
of what might enter unseen
into your small completely insignificant

white nostrils, what sex, what
disease, what death, what
unwanted desire.

But for no reason at all, certainly
not out of bravery, you walk into it
anyway, and when you see the first brown breast,
the first woman and child,
the dark nipples like pieces of dark gold,

it takes your breath away, the pure brown
against the pure white blouses,
and when you see the next
and the next, the large bodies,
the large breasts,
it seems the milk is running
down the streets, rivers of milk
and suckling children,

and the backs bent and loaded
with children and wool
and fruits and on every street
women give themselves to children
like wild fruit. Some children lie spread

across the laps of their mothers
sleeping but holding
the nipple tight in their mouths
as if it were a dream,
or candy or God, and you forget
to think about not breathing
and it all enters you, the smell
of wet straw, exhaust
of cars and broken down buses,
the sweat and breath of foreign bodies
and even the smell of wool enters you,
and the smell of money
and hands old and cracked with barter
and the smell of beggars with faces

so mangled they no longer look like faces
but puzzles put together
the wrong way, so that
you cannot look or breathe again,

and you cannot believe there is a god
until you hear the words, *granadillas,*
*semillas, naranjas.* You are beginning
to notice how the clouds are sinking
into the Andes like a woman into her man,

the mountains with their strong backs
and eyes like stones or stones
like eyes, you can no longer tell
which, and without warning
Christ is paraded through the streets
painted and bleeding
and pierced, the nails clear
as the smells now, it is

the Christ of your childhood
all lit up with flowers and lights
like a Christmas tree,

there are singing people
and dogs and a band in the street,
sellers and buyers, backs and hands and breasts,
and long after it is all over
you are still standing there breathing
the thin night air,

and there is only one man left
with one flute, his black hair
pulled back and braided to the waist.

He is standing in a doorway to a place
you cannot enter,

and suddenly you notice how high
the clouds have taken you,
how the sky sings, how
heavy the breath of god.

## ◎◎ *Why I Went into the Jungle*

Because I wanted to become blind again,
as at birth, because I wanted to feel
darkness heavy and wet around me
like sex or death, the molecules of night
dancing in my skin like jaguars.
I wanted to lose my way
to light because truth
loves darkness, I wanted to be
where I didn't know the names
of things to learn them
as blood learns the way of veins.
I wanted to fall into the malarial waters,
to be born again, a thing alive
and dark with knowing.

## ❧❧ *Jungle*

I have looked southward with the eyes of my people,
eyes like fires that consume and possess, southward
past the swollen and empty belly of the Americas,
ever southward, ever lower, to where
I felt it once long ago, to where
I know it lives, hot and lush
like a thing almost not there,
a breath, the screech of a great
animal caged and starving and desperate,
I have looked, but I have not seen it,


have not found the tangle and knot
of tree and vine and plant, nor
the green pumping of vine on vine
and tree on tree, filling and feeding
the air as if it were food;
I have looked for but have not found
lianas twisted and supple as arteries,
have not found howler or woolly or white-
faced monkeys screeching or barking
their anguish or joy, no
strangler figs with their roots
that have learned how to lengthen
and thicken and surround the mother tree
until they become her, no epiphytes,
intelligent plants that have learned
to live without roots, happy
relationship that does not consume
or invite consumption.

There are no giant trees
that startle with their girth and breadth
and height, and are terrifying in their hugeness
and the hugeness of their solitude,
their leaves like immense regrets
that tower and block the sun so that all
is dark and fertile as sorrow underneath.


There is nowhere to be lost now,
no way to disappear into a center
whose exits and entrances are obscured,
nowhere to bathe in the sound, color
and smell of the *other*.
Everything has become familiar,
the way in as clear as the way out,
the trails paved and smooth as a road
that follows a pipeline.


There are no birds
of paradise, no trees of banana
or guava or papaya, no passion-
fruit or bread fruit, no jungle
mango or garlic, no clouds
of mist or rain or humidity that
hang heavy as sex in the air,


and though you walk the ruined veins
of it, mud clinging to you like sun,
you will not find the champagne-cup
mushrooms that used to grow here, or the small,
delicate frogs like translucent hearts that loved

to rest here, you will not find yellow-headed vultures,
there will be no snake birds,
or resplendent quetzals, who,
with the intelligence of all great animals,
cannot live in captivity,
you will not find the clear-winged
butterfly, proof that the physical
can exist and not be seen, nor
the wasps whose beating wings
sound the tramp of waves of foolish gods,


nor will you see the Jesus birds that walk on water,
or the clouds of blue and yellow macaws
or emerald toucans or parrots
or the blue-necked fruit crow—


no Limoncochas, lakes of lime colored waters,
or rivers of coffee and lemon and tar,
no Hoatzins or Bell birds,
no caimons in their dark waters of grief
and knowledge, their eyes
red as new volcanic rock
in the invisible night.


Gone, too, the mushroom that looks
like a woman's nipple, its petals
that release their musty spores
like a breath when you press
the center button gently,
as an insect lighting its whole
body on a sunning woman's naked breast.

No natives, and their knowledge
to heal the terrors of the body
and the nightmares of the soul
as invisible as they.


And you will not be able
to imagine what you cannot see:
the beloved as a jungle river,
lips, breath and body snaking and winding,
almost touching, almost stopping,
moving so slowly it hardly seems
to move at all.

                        Nor will you be able
to think like a jungle, to imagine your body
as jungle, a tangle
of intestines and guts and shining
corpuscles and muddy vines and sorrowing leaves
and arteries and bones and marrows,
the infinite variety of skins and textures
and scents and bruises like flowers and fungus
and algae that grow in all our closed-in
dark places, your legs
the skinny white trunks of jungle trees,
your heart a golden toad,
your feet buttresses.
The way you kill yourself daily,
the little deaths of pollution
and sweet drugs.

And though you look for the *other* as one dying
of thirst you will not find it
until you wake one morning,
find your back hardened with the knowledge
of the dying, the truly ancient—
you will perhaps wear a shawl as the old ones do,
but even then you may not see, as we hardly ever see
that which is important until it is too late,
how like a great tree you are,
how the shawl covers you like a bromeliad,
how exotic you are,
how resplendent,
how nearly extinct.

## ◎◎   *Learning a Language*

*—for my father*

1

In this lightless room flooded with tongues,
his own is too heavy to lift.
We ask if he can form his words better.
*I'm yearning,* he says, meaning
*learning.* Hands strapped down,
chest strapped, too much ammonia
in the brain, he is in the dark country
of the tongueless.


Meanwhile we learn the new language
of his body, the one, unlike his, that is
clear, precise: catheter, IV, feeding tube,
respirator, suction tube, pre-coma X-ray.
But there are no words in this language
for speech, there is nothing to make
him speak out of that country
in the voice we used to know.


And nothing changes, time marks the days
he lies in half-life. *Endure,*
the doctors whisper with their paraphernalia,
*breathe.*

2

I mark time by taking up another language;
it is useful where I live. I study obsessively:
there are rules of pronunciation to follow,
progress can be made. *Tengo ojos castaños,* I write
over and over in my notebook, *tengo pelo
castaño,* until I get it right. The *d* in *miedo*
is always pronounced like the *th* in *Father,*
*anaranjado* always means *orange.*

A nation breeds in my mouth, in his.

## ⊘⊘  *Cholera*

*1*

It is a woman with unwashed hands,
her life singing in the dirt
under her nails, the Angel
almost appearing behind her
as a dark wind or bird.
She is eating an unwashed
fruit cut open like the head
of a cow severed from its body,
the two parts studded with glistening
murmuring flies, those
*cherubim* of the physical world.
The fruit is large and melon-like,
sweet, and the juice runs down
her lips and hands and arms
like the blood of Christ
as she looks up at the anguished sky,
the gathering of medieval gods.

*2*

And none will be saved in these mountains
where corn dries and waits patiently
as death, and wool is shorn and spun
and hung to dry, where
soup boils in angry black pots
that are big but not big enough,
where houses are floorless and eyeless.

The black cherubim fly freely
in and out where Jesus is taped
to the wall like a pinup girl,
where mountains grow older
and greener with each death,
the many voices becoming rock
and soil. No one will be saved
despite the sacred waterfalls
and eucalyptus groves, despite
the sounds of wings of thousands of angels,
despite the sacred pools where spirits
are strengthened, it is not spirits
but bodies which are ill, no,
despite the mushrooms that turn into God
when you eat them, He will not be found,

only the women in the waters
that thread and separate this land,
the women, feet and ankles up to hips
in the unrelenting rushing water,
beating clothes against rocks,
beating and beating until the rocks
weep, until the rocks become heads
of cows that bleed through all
the watery streets where children
play and drink and defecate—
no one will be saved,
not the proud or the blind,
or even the drunk, you can
smell it in the air,
in the colors of the waters,
in the skins of the fruits
and the skins of hands,
and the beautiful baked, unwashed feet.

It is in the buses that take Death
from town to town without
making Him pay. The lesser angels,
silent and hungry, wait
like the corn to be dried,
emptied of all their liquid,
wait like the wool to dry,
to be born again.


3


When the Angel finally
comes, first the bodies will give up
all their water. They will hemorrhage
themselves into the River, it does not take long,
the Angel is merciful in this way,
and their voices will go, for voice
is nothing but water, and the blood
will thicken to tar and finally stop
moving because without water
nothing moves but the dark River
that rushes on with its deafening voices
we do not hear.

## ◎◎  *Tropical*


When you first descend into it
you can feel its warm equatorial
breath, sweet and lost, breath
of things becoming other things.
Fruit and banana smell, omniscient
and overripe as God, *piñas* and oranges,
*limónes*—

A heaviness comes
with the moisture
trapped like a lost soul,
a thing fermenting. Ferns and vines
strangle like a flowering of love,
and you walk deeper into it,
the air almost as heavy as you
now, wise with water.

One moment you are what you have always been,
the next there's something fruital
and empty in you.

Mist, rain and waterfall,
all that is green and growing.
Fruit, vine and dying.
What waits in the heat,
perfumed and dark,
close to ground.

## ☯☯ *Mayan Ruins and the Y Summer Camp Counselor*

*—on hearing that my son's YMCA counselor has been arrested and convicted on three counts of sexual abuse of a child, and that the police want to interview my son*


As I walk these ruins I'm thinking
about how much there is that we don't know,
how much we allow to remain unexcavated,
the cost of archaeologists and their teams
and equipment too great for countries
where the greatest ruins lie,
or maybe we're afraid of what we might find,
what relations, what blood sacrifices,
what darkness that doesn't yet
have a name—it's enough, perhaps,
to have discovered the heaps of skulls
severed from the bones of bodies,
it's enough, the ruined altars cleaned
of mud and grit to reveal the carefully etched
scenes of bound captives.

There are things that even I, who love
the dark overmuch, do not want to know,
things that, no matter how well said
can never be beautiful.

There is a smell that pervades the jungle here,
whether it is the smell of ruin, or of the long dead
and decayed opened to light, or
of something else I cannot tell.
It is a smell looking to root itself,
it is as ugly as the ruins are beautiful,
as if a protection of them somehow,
*go away, go away.*

The ancient rocks and trees are caught
in each other, each trying to claim the other,
each trying to root in the other.
It's hard to stop seeds from lodging
themselves in the cracks of stones,
the ancient temples and palaces will always crack
somewhere, the seed will lodge itself,
begin to grow, and as it grows
the rock will crack more and more, as when
a grown man enters a small child, until
the roots and stone are caught together,
inseparable. The stone thinks it's soil
because the roots tell it so.

I am thinking about how
the shadows of the ancient priests
on top of the temples
must have grown
as the sun dropped lower in the sky
behind them, how their shadows
must have covered the shadows
of the people below,
how such shadows must have
seemed god-like to the peasants
small as children below.

The jungle mourns and weeps,
the cycle of darkness begins again,
each new day bound victims tremble
on crumbling altars, kings look on
with their useless faces,
and I do not know what to do
with my grief, it hangs on me
like a thing wanting to be put down,
to be made useful, wanting to be said,
for the ruined children,
the helpless gods.

## ☯ *Coastal*

You have been too long land locked,
too long in the libraries of scrub
and cactus, droughtened, predictable
lands without the smell of your birth.

Maybe it is the wind
that suddenly awakens you
like a slap it lifts
the ocean to you, it is
the smell of your mother,
of some infinite longing, of sex,
of shells and bones sun-white
in their death and crab smell.
Sea salt, fish and the sands
with their infinitesimally
small bits of broken shells
and guts and bodies and hearts.
Sea smell of something dead.

Familiar, like family,
this haphazard meeting of
indifferent land, indifferent sea,
The sand, milk,
the coast your body.

## ❀❀ *Postcard about the Body*

Poor birds that don't have lips,
they do what they can, dancing
and pointing their inefficient hard beaks
to the sky—or maybe the poverty

is ours for being cursed with lips
that weep and crack for lack of kissing
when the beloved is an ocean away.
Beaks would be easier, would listen
to reason—

On these islands, all the birds
are mating or fucking or building nests,
and it is the greatest sorrow
to even open my legs casually
without you.

Tonight I shall put on my great colored coat
as the frigate bird
wears his inflated throat,
I shall fly across the ocean
in my foolish, wingless body,
in my coat of throats—
I shall fly to your fleshy featherless body,
to your lips, generous as blood and salt,
full and round as mortality.

## ✪✪  *What the Sea Turtles Know*

The mothers know to come out
of the sea under cover of dark,
they know to bury their eggs
under dark sand, and the turtle
embryos grow in that dark,
learn it as I have not yet learned mine,
suckle it in place of a mother.
Lain and warmed to being
in dark, they know to wait for night
to be born to the sea
where their kind await them.

I have seen frigate birds and hawks
circling for hours the great nests
of sea turtles on days
when clouds chum and joke
with the light, so that day
seems night come early
and the hatchlings make
their fatal mistranslation
of light and rise from their dark nests
thinking to make it that short way
to sea, only to be plucked into light,
into the clouds, accomplices
of the grinning murderer, day.

The ones who wait for the real dark,
the ones who make it to the sea
know that darkness is all desire
and that desire, life—
and so they return
to the dark waters of the seas
where they were conceived,
to lagoons lipped with mangroves
their roots hard and straight as bars,
and there the turtles love
and mate in their own way.

Creatures of light,
we do not see much of them,
only now and again their huge
intelligent heads that lift
out of waters for the briefest
of breaths, only the trails
the new mothers leave
from sea to nest and back,
the way between their thousands of eggs,
their wondrous dark.

## At the Equator

There is no lingering here—morning
light does not make itself known
slowly—there are no long moments
lying in bed, eyes closed, slightly
awake, the darkness become
only slightly less dark,
then gray dark, a shade of pink,
the slow realization that
it is *becoming light*.
It is that I miss,
the light is here, then gone,
no nonsense about it.

My husband
never slept a night alone
after the separation,
some gentle head, immediate
as a flashlight on the pillow next to his.

I want to live far from here
where knowledge is slow
in coming, where
it changes and leaves
with the slowness of old age.

I can stand no longer
the equatorial sadness of Spring,
the beds heavy with body,
the sunken pillows crying out
their fear of emptiness.

## ◎◎  *Guatemala*

When I think of Guatemala
I think of us, how you said
Lake Atitlán was in my eyes,
calm and startlingly beautiful
— as ruthless things always are—
though you did not say that:
you cannot imagine
that beauty and terror could reside
in the same place.

You love me like a tourist.
You don't see the desperate men
with rifles that run in my blood,
the disemboweled children and disappeared
fathers and husbands in my eyes—
just like here, in this place,
you do not see
how the gorgeous land reels,
lurches with death.

## Song Against the Conquistadores

Let us sing with quenas and charangos,
let us play until our fingers bleed,
let us beat the skins of drums, let us beat
the flesh of wood until it cries out,
let us pleasure zampoñas wildly as if
they were the beloved and this the last
holy night of lovemaking,
let us raise the dead with voices
with mouths and fingers, let us sing
the mountains, bleak
and beautiful, let us sing our tongue,
let us sing the tongues of our murderers.

Let us weep for the voices gone,
for animals that will not survive us,
for plants, let us weep for insects
dying, their voices in the voices of the dead already
let us weep let us weep let us weep let us
sing wild sadness let us climb higher and higher
to the top of the mountains to the top of grief,
let the song be rain be grace,
let the song be rain be grace,
let it rain like spears, like beasts like blood
like tears let it rain like memory like history
like pain like beauty like rain.

## ◎◎   *The Weight of My Country*

South America, underworld
of underworlds where jungles swim
and mountains drown, where
oceans of fish follow like my own
past or that of my country—

I swear I cannot tell,
when North America bears down,
if it is a mother birthing
or smothering her young,
but the weight of my country
is in me like a shadow
I cannot disengage,
its manipulations, its assassinations,
its greedy fingerings,
my hands heavy with shadow
even as I disown it.

Here, all is underwater,
a vibrant and dying
ocean where those who live
speak the logic of starving fish.

Like the fish of their great jungle waters,
I cannot read the shadow in the shallows
towards which this country moves,
mouth open.

*II*

*Here I am, safely returned over those peaks from a journey*
*far more beautiful than anything I had hoped for or*
    *imagined—*
*how is it that this safe return brings such regret?*

*Peter Matthiessen*

## ◎◎  *In the Garden of Eden*

No one tells much about it,
but there were vultures in the Garden of Eden.
Turkey vultures, to be exact.
Dark eagles, they would soar like gods,
voiceless, their wings held out in blessing,
their unfeathered heads the red-jewels
of the sky of the garden.

They were vegetarian then.
There were no roadside kills,
no bones to pick, no dead flesh to bloom, ripen.

And they were happy.
They could not imagine
what they would become.

## ◉◉ *Big Fish*

The ones that grow large and thrive,
the ones that have once tasted the hook,
the mouth-scarred ones, do not linger
in unclouded waters. They have learned
to live in deeper pools,
water cold as knives, weedy
with dark food, murky
amniotic fluid—

Wise fish, with gills
that open like wounds,
passing the tragic waters
through their bodies,
turning grief to oxygen.

## ൦൦ *Fisherman*

To listen with hands and eyes
for the deep, unseen mouthing—
if I could have the faith of the fisherman
I would rip out my heart muscle,
sink a hook into its joyous pulsing,
sing it out on a long line,
and wait for the great dark.

## ⊚⊚ *Hoping for Disaster*

The days stretch out,
changeless, efficient
as a familiar recipe.

Your life is too sober.
You have the wary eyes
of a recovered alcoholic,
though you are not one.

Everything repeats itself but passion,
which has run out like a creek
in late summer. Your eyes widen and bag
like an owl in the morning. You ask
your reflection *what do you know*
that you look like this.
Your heart weakens but does not stop—
it is as if you have some flu
of the heart, or you have lost
it, the heart, somewhere.

They told you to stockpile provisions here,
in case the creek floods and you can't get out.
So you've put your mother—six cans of tomatoes—
into the pantry. Her face beams from the outside
of the cans: *eat me without guilt.*
Your father is in the whiskey bottle
hidden behind the cans of corn that are your sister.
He is half gone, you have drunk much of him
the last nights here. And you don't know
where your brother is, perhaps lost with your heart,

and today you have decided to build a raft
with some dead branches and twine,
you are hoping for disaster,
something huge, something to destroy
everything.

## ⊚⊚ *School Bus, Seven* A.M.


Three women are talking at the end of a dirt road.
It is October, so it is still dark
although the sun is threatening.

They clench and unclench themselves
in the morning light, they worry their fingers
as if the air were dough of a bread
that will never rise,
or rise dark and bitter.

Before they part each will stare down
the lightening road where a yellow bus
slouches off, its belly stuffed with children.

## ᯤᯤ  *Night Sky with Clothesline*

Night pours itself like grace over the ocean,
and a melon-white moon
spills its fruital light over it all.
I can see from my window
what seems to be nature's perfection,
the perfect light and sky,
the perfect ocean and waves—

It is boring, all this beauty,
and I'm happy that a clothesline
is strung across the balcony
outside the window, that it cuts
through the stomach of night
like a deep scar, that an empty blouse
hangs on the line like something lost or forgotten,
waving in the perfect night its wisdom.

*◎◎   The Headlights of God*

The world is still dark
with night's wisdom
but for my headlights,
which light the dirt road ahead
like God's shining.

A rabbit trips
into the light, bounds ahead.
He bounds and bounds, faster and faster;
we follow in the car. Sometimes
he stops to look behind,
then bounds ever faster ahead.
My son doubles with laughter,
urges me to drive faster.

I think how heavy the rabbit must be
with terror—he has forgotten
or can no longer see
the dark brush on either side,

he has forgotten or has not yet learned
that the thing lighting the way
is almost always the thing
from which you must escape.

## ೞ೦  *Losing Faith*


Her robe was the sky on a spring night,
edged in gold, it hung on her
in folds that sighed about her body.
Her face was all I knew of beauty
then, flawless, earthly,
with flushed cheeks and peach-dark lips
open and almost breathing,
giving and taking back at once
hope.                              .

Her hair was the color of young oak
and fell in thick waves around
her face where it disappeared like God
into her mantle. The folds of it
and the robe met at the neck,
obscuring the rest of her hair,
and I loved this small mystery about her.

She stood on a globe of the world
and was queened with a moon
the color of honey behind her head.
Her eyes were blue, cold and warm both,
her feet were bare, naked-pink,
and crushed a colored snake
that muscled about the world.
There were always candles lit
at her altar that gave off
a burnt perfume I loved.
If I crossed my eyes
they looked like stars.

I will never forget that Sunday
we arrived for mid-morning Mass
to find that all the statues had been washed
of color and painted brown.
The priest explained it was to remind us
they were symbols really,
that we had been taking these statues
much too seriously, that we needed to remember
they stood for something beyond themselves.

It was never the same after that,
the poor washed brown of her statue
reminded me of roaches, or shit,
or when we had to eat beans and rice
for a whole week once, or the generic
cans of peanut butter daddy brought
home from the army. I couldn't look
at her anymore.

And now, when I reach for the precise moment
of the larger doubt, its furtive dawning
in my child heart, the first knot of a wound
that would sing darkness awake,
it is the death of that statue I think of,
first sign that maybe what they had taught me
was wrong, that there were choices,
mistakes could be made.

## ൭ৎ  *Backyard, November*

The backyard is haunted
with the failures of summer.

You look around and don't know
what you could have been, then.

Here are the sad signposts
of what should have grown—
watermelon, tomato, a type
of bean—

and there, in the corner, the remains
of a sign the kids made for a club
house, never built—*no grownups allowed.*

Here, the careful edge fencing
of some mad person around a garden
that was never planted.

No one knows why we announce so much
that we do not finish, except
November, who marches in after
every good idea, calm and sure
as an adult who knows better.

Imagine the moment between blindness and first sight,
a kind of color-fire you cannot interpret.
Hands are blotches of color with holes of light.
There are horrifying realizations—
that you have a face, an appearance.

A book about the wonders of eye surgery
also tells of unexpected failures:
a newly-sighted man begs to have vision
taken away again, threatens
to tear out his eyes.

A cow bellows in the distance.
We sit on calm sofas, watch boys
with faces fresh as eggs
talk of war.

A cricket has been singing day and night
behind the refrigerator.
Soon he will drop from exhaustion.
It is dark back there, and warm—
he can not tell that it is day, winter.

## ☯ *Flooded*

The creek is flooded to river
with water, swollen like a fresh bruise.
Bodies float down, uninterrupted
with faces turned down
and arms outstretched
like Christ's.

I am like this: flooded to river
with death, death my subject
as water is the creek's,
death the beloved we can
never know though
we are swollen with the waters
of wanting, death, the past,
death, my relative, my father
and mother, the face of my brother,
death's blood in me,
death flooding me
filling the valleys, rising
in the hills of me—

I do not know why we are not crazed,
all of us, at the death of just
one person. I do not know
how we have survived all these
years, all these deaths
that flood us like music or breath.

The creek is beautiful like this,
terrifying and mesmerizing
as fire gone wild.

## Flooded Crossing

That month the rain was strange,
coming when we hadn't expected it—
ten cold inches during one week
in January. I had almost forgotten
what fear was like until we faced
the wall of shouting water,
swelling, flooding over the low
water crossing, blocking the
way to the house.

Stupid, I tried to ford the creek
at the crossing, refusing
to admit there was something
I couldn't do. The sucking water
turned me back before disaster,
but I stared for a long time
at my failure.

How could I tell my son what I saw
when he asked what I was staring at?
How could I tell him I understood
again, my brother, that last time
he pumped too much stuff into
his arms: the rushing of the creek,
something worth one's respect,
something to be afraid of.

## ◎◎  *August Fire*

All that morning I had wanted to write about breasts,
pouting breasts, heavy and sweet with age,
or small breasts that tip upwards like swollen wine
        skeins,
young breasts ignorant of mouths,
breasts of new mothers hard with milk,
I had wanted to write about the weeping of breasts,
the scarring of breasts, breasts that smell of onions,
breasts that sway to the waist in joy or aching,
breasts that disappear to stretched skin,

so when I looked out the window at first
I didn't see flames but breasts,
their milk like fire in the hot windy air.
The heat that moved like a wall
was only the warmth of breasts on a cold night,
a place to keep hands warm.
Fire dressed the cedar tree near the house
then, like a lover, stripped it.
Flames licked the tip like tongues
would a nipple.

I don't know how long I saw breasts instead of fire,
how long it took me to phone for help—
when I finally sat down to write
it was night, my hands were black.

They tell me grass comes up greener
after a fire. I am happy to hear this,
for the land lies soaking in a black milk.

47

I look out over the waste of oak, cedar
and high brush and grass, my eyes
full of grief. Only the prickly pear,
that stout cactus, was saved
by its inner moisture. It bears
its red fruit like nipples hard bitten
and swollen. Its bodies, thick and green,
breast the blackened land.

## ❦❦  *The Shrimp Peelers*

The table is dark, and the room—
only a bulb, naked, hangs
like the skull of some small
animal, lighting the room
where shrimp are peeled
by small, foreign hands.

It is nothing to peel shrimp
for oneself, but I have stood
here for hours, like southern women
before me, alone in a kitchen,
and peeled the shrimp
for the family to eat.
I have thought, as I peeled,
about those who measure
their lives by the piles
of empty shells, the hourly
wages of the hands,

the small dignities
of a job well done and honestly.
Here, heads are twisted off
like the mangled names
of immigrants, the naked
skins, the gut veins stripped out,
none left after twenty years
of this, oh,

but the beauty of the hands
of the shrimp peelers,
brown, black and woman mostly,

the hands that do the work
that needs to be done,
the moneyless hands, slow
to earn their bloody wage,
oh hands of my mother
and grandmother, oh holy
nights of hands peeling shrimp,
oh wise hands and forgiving
of the repetitious task.

The piles of shells and heads
and legs rise like antediluvian mountains,
the dark waste of their song
reeks through the ages.

## In the Garden of Eden, Thinking
of the Beloved

There is nothing here that does not remind me of him,
the mountains wordless and rich with everything,

the water, so clear you can see deep into it, but not to
bottom,

and the flowers, the white wild flowers I saw today
reminded me of the time driving through New
Mexico when we noticed all at once how quiet it
was, got out of the car, and he found some flowers, picked them and awkwardly gave them to me
saying *I'm glad you spoke your mind last night.*

I kept them until they turned to colored dust.

And the time in New York when he bought lavender
tulips for us from a store in the Village and we
made love with those tulips in bed with us, put-
ting them between my breasts and thighs, touching them to our mouths, his mouth, oh I cannot
speak of his mouth.

In Texas it was honeysuckle we piled on the bed, the
hot sweet smell of August in them, wrapping the
vines around us, pressing the nectar on my
nipples where he could lick it off, and wine, yes
there was wine then too, that red Cabernet we
liked so much, and I kissed him with wine in my
mouth.

And even the sky is him as the sun reaches long and
    low along the horizon like red flames of his hair,

and the fruit, how could I not think of him when I eat
    the raspberries and blueberries and oranges and
    plums, the cold bright and dusty colors filling my
    mouth like him,

and thinking of him eating, how he is always the last
    to pick up his fork and the last to put it down,

and I am in the garden flowerless and kissless, naked
    without his mouth,

and my eyes cannot make anything stop.

## ❧❧ *Thinking about Herbs*

This is how I rise in you,
this green breath of words,
this pungent aroma that
cries out until you bring the crushed
things to your face, inhale deeply.

## ⊙⊚  *The Erotic*

I scatter corn around the yard and wait
for them to come at dawn and dusk,
two or three does together with twin
fawns, gangly, falling down. Sometimes
bucks come—alone, suspicious, male.
They are young, mostly. I watch them
in the dark of my own house
with binoculars, like a lonely woman
might watch a man undress
from a far window.

Bob says that the erotic
is hardly ever sexual, only
when we're lucky.
Oh how I want that luck!
I wait for the moment I love best
when their white tails go up
in warning, erect and full
as a loved one you stroke
but don't let come.

ᕮᕯᕳ   *Want*


Two young bucks come daily to eat.
Their nubs of antlers are almost
pushing through skin, it must hurt,
like new teeth almost erupting through
gums, the gums sore and red and full
of tooth. This is what it is like
to want you. Long days while
the gleaming white thing grows
larger under skin that weeps daily,
wanting to be broken.

⊚⊚ *Not Asking*

The black stockings wait,
like me, for someone
to enter them, build them.

I have no voice for this,
that voice in my gut torn
out some time ago, now
there must be one
who knows the marrow
of my desire, the genetics
of my lust, the body
as voice, this deep black
nothing, never
reaching out,
always

opening.

## ꙮ *Christmas Night, After Making Love*

The clock's voice,
the wet mushroom smell singing
in my thighs: repetition.

Christmas again,
and I am empty with joy.

Everyone sleeps, holds hope
as if it were time.

My mouth is warm, meat
cools in the kitchen.

## ◎◎ *Just Say No to Insect Sex*

If there is a god, he is the one
responsible for insect sex.
How his divine brain must have
rippled like a big fish
when he thought of their writhing
at that moment of sexual prayer,
the fatal joining, the great
thrusting that is loss and gift.

He must have known that creatures
would evolve, that they would addict themselves
in time, to his dark symbiosis.

And he must have known that men
would become jealous of insects,
especially the mantid's fermata,
that they would fall, some of them,
into darkness, that they would invent
silk ties and belts for women
to wrap around their throats,
that they would close their eyes
perhaps as the mantid closes his,
at the moment of strangulation.

I remember that sometimes
when we make love
I am a host of god-thoughts,
crueler than any insect.

Poor insects, they have
no morals with which to dress,
only a mattress of indifference
to lie upon. They are bloodless,
and wear skeletons like coats.

Ours are hidden
under flesh and moral blood
that doesn't understand
its own dark rushing,
doesn't know how to say
without judgment
that there are places horrific in light
to which we swarm at night.

## ⊙⊘ *Blindfolds, Ropes*

In this place of utter light and vastness
I have lit my soul with searchlights,
and cannot tell the limits of my fear or joy.

The truth is I miss your blindfolds and ropes,
those gifts I left with you.

In light you are a gangly, red-nosed
Englishman; in dark you become
the Beloved—all breath, skin and tongue—
a truth no light would reveal.

Tonight when I close my eyes
the sky will fill with lovers
binding the wrists of lovers,
the night will tie its blindfold
over the earth's eyes, and I will
dream of how to speak—oh

kiss me with lips I have to imagine;
hold me in a room I can't escape.

## ꩜ *Angels*

Sometimes I think all angels are dark,
fallen like faith from the porcelain hand
of some god, all angels are angels of november,
of coming winter, of mutilations, addictions,
dead children and boys killed at war,
angels of mourning, they come singing dirges,
they are the ones who take grief into them,
it is what gives them shape, it is what makes them
so dark—it fills them like sails of ships that
will never return home, or bellies of women
who are pregnant and starving. I love how their song
floats down on clouded nights, that dark grace
like rain pelting the parched souls,
the empty tongues.

## ೞಶ *Spring*

*1*

I work in the garden
most mornings now,
cutting and pruning, wrestling
weeds with their roots
that grip and vein
the dark beautiful soil,
want to pull me there, and I think
of the man who owned this house
for sixty years. It's mine now,
he died at eighty-eight last spring,
after working in the garden.
He put his tools up, cleaned off
the push mower, went into the bathroom,
had a massive stroke.

His Camellias have been blooming
since January. I remember how shocked
I was to see the bushes burst into flower
with the weather so cold.

My clitoris is a tight bud most days,
a fist, a nut. It refuses to open unless
the weather is right. I do rain dances, pound
the ground, but it will not
open unless there is much rain and sun,
the *right kind* of sun—

2

The bulbs of these irises he planted
are just opening now to rain
and early spring sun, to a new face,
new clippers.

His azaleas are blooming too,
flaunting their gorgeous stuff
like an old photograph of me.
All that nakedness, all that color.

And the roses. I let the flowers
stay on the bushes until the petals
are as worn as my face these days.
When they drop to earth they drop
like prayers, exhausted with living.

All this, all, *he* planted,
and I feel oddly intimate with him,
as if his hands touched my breasts
when I reach to prune a branch,
or bend to cut a flower.
I swear sometimes the soil
itself sobs when I work it,
as if I were trying to make
his tough old penis rise,
as if his body were alive
in the soil. His hands grip,
his fingers worm and root

the good dirt, I cannot avoid them.
The broken earth, like a body
prepared for fucking or love
or something I do not yet know.


3


As if just thinking of someone
could be like rain and sun,
could bring one to flower.

Gray hairs sprout like weeds
in my head. I comb them,
I love them.

Sheryl St. Germain's poetry has received several
awards, including a grant from The National
Endowment for the Arts, a Dobie-Paisano Fellowship,
a grant from the Texas Council on the Arts and the Ki
Davis Award from the Aspen Writers Foundation. Her
previous books include *The Mask of Medusa*, *Going
Home*, and *Making Bread at Midnight*. She lives in
Galesburg, Illinois, where she teaches creative writing
and literature at Knox College.